DREAMWORKS
Spirit
RIDING FREE

Riding Academy
Race

DreamWorks Spirit Riding Free © 2020 DreamWorks Animation LLC.
All Rights Reserved.
Illustrations by Maine Diaz

Cover design by Ching Chan. Cover illustration by Maine Diaz.

Little, Brown and Company
Hachette Book Group
1290 Avenue of the Americas, New York, NY 10104
Visit us at LBYR.com

First Edition: August 2020

Little, Brown and Company is a division of Hachette Book Group, Inc. The Little, Brown name and logo are trademarks of Hachette Book Group, Inc.

The publisher is not responsible for websites (or their content) that are not owned by the publisher.

Library of Congress Cataloging-in-Publication Data

Names: Deutsch, Stacia, author. | Diaz, Maine, illustrator.

Title: Riding academy race / Stacia Deutsch ; illustrated by Maine Diaz.

Other titles: Spirit riding free (Television program)

Description: New York : Little, Brown and Company, 2020. | Inspired by the Netflix animated television series Spirit riding free. | Audience: Ages 6-10. | Summary: "The PALs and their new friends at the Palomino Riding Academy keep having disagreements! With the help of a scavenger hunt, can they figure out how to work together as a team?"—Provided by publisher.

Identifiers: LCCN 2019058449 | ISBN 9780316460255 (paperback) | ISBN 9780316460248 (ebook) | ISBN 9780316460231 (ebook other)

Classification: LCC PZ7.D4953 Ri 2020 | DDC [Fic]—dc23

LC record available at https://lccn.loc.gov/2019058449

Printed in the United States of America

LSC-C

10 9 8 7 6 5 4 3 2 1

OFFICIAL
MARK OF
SPIRIT

DreamWorks

Spirit

RIDING FREE

Riding Academy Race

Stacia Deutsch

Illustrated by **Maine Diaz**

Little, Brown and Company
New York Boston

Chapter 1

"I wish you had asked before using my tack, Lyds." Priya was calm but disappointed.

"It was an emergency," Lyds tried to explain. "I was in a hurry. I thought you'd understand."

Priya said, "Had you come to my quarters, I'd have been delighted to grant my approval." The dorm rooms at Palomino Bluffs Academy were directly above the horse stables. "And one more thing—it's customary when borrowing someone else's tack to bring it back in pristine condition," Priya continued. "The leather should be brightened with saddle soap and shimmering oil. I do love it when the leather shines." She shivered happily at the thought. "It's delightful."

"I was in a hurry—" Lyds said again.

"Nevertheless," Priya interrupted.

That was when Pru, Abigail, and Lucky walked into the stables.

Everyone who lived in the first-year Foal Canter House could hear Lyds and Priya's back-and-forth discussion about when it was okay to borrow someone's tack. They'd been discussing the issue, going around in circles, for nearly an hour.

Lucky leaned over to her friends and whispered, "Should we do something?" She waved her hand toward the stalls. "The horses don't like conflict."

Spirit's ears were pricked. Chica Linda's eyes bulged. They both snorted.

Boomerang yawned.

"Boomerang doesn't mind," Abigail said. "He's used to Snips and me arguing all the time. In fact, Boomerang would probably start snoring if they started shouting."

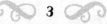

3

"Priya's not really the shouting type," Lucky said. She paused to consider the issue. "I think Lydia should have asked to borrow the tack."

"Maybe Lyds really needed it," Abigail countered. "There are two sides to every horse's harness."

"I'm sure Priya and Lyds will work it out," Pru said.

Lucky swung one arm over Pru's shoulder and wrapped the other around Abigail. "You're right. Best friends *always* make up."

"Borrowing tack is a small thing to forgive!" Abigail said. "They'll definitely get over it. Remember that time you threw away my ice-cream cone before I finished it? I forgave both of you, and that was a *huge* thing!"

"The ice cream was melting!" Pru said.

"*And* dripping all over Aunt Cora's clean floor," Lucky added.

"That's not my fault! I had to return that library book before the library closed! So

maybe I got a little delayed when I was picking a new book. The library has *so* many choices—can you really blame me? Anyway, you both *promised* to watch my ice cream while I was gone. You *broke* that promise." Abigail peeled herself away from Lucky's arm. She stepped back. "Actually, I don't think I *do* forgive either of you." She pointed at Pru, then at Lucky, and announced, "*Someone* owes me ice cream."

Boomerang whinnied.

"Thanks for reminding me, Boomerang!" Abigail gave him a pat on the nose. "He says the ice cream should have extra rainbow sprinkles."

"We'll do you one better," Lucky assured

Abigail. "Next time we're in Miradero, we'll get you a whole sundae!"

"With whipped cream *and* rainbow sprinkles," Pru agreed.

Abigail stepped back in line with her friends and linked arms. "In that case, I guess I can forgive you again." She smiled and tipped her head toward Priya and Lyds, who were still tensely discussing the situation. "See? That's how PALs make up." She licked her lips. "Deliciously."

"We should get out of here. Lyds and Priya are friends. They'll figure out what to do on their own," Lucky said. "Let's go ride in the ramada."

Pru glanced out of the barn. She looked past the white fence that circled the riding ring and asked, "We're signed up for this time slot, aren't we?"

"I wrote our names on the sign-up sheet myself," Abigail said. She went to a wall in the barn where a clipboard hung. She pointed. "There. It says 'PALs.'" Abigail checked the clock. "We're right on time. Let's start practicing our jumps. I'm going to teach Boomerang to jump higher than ever before! He's always wanted to touch the clouds."

"You know, you've touched clouds before," Lucky said as her friends began tacking up their horses. "Fog is a kind of cloud."

"He'll jump higher than fog, then," Abigail said. "Over the clouds!"

"I don't think Boomerang will be touching *any* clouds today." Pru raised her voice because Priya and Lyds were still debating the rules of borrowing tack. "The

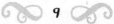

BUDs are already riding in the arena."

The girls and their horses rushed out of the barn to find Bebe, Ursula, and Daphne in the ring, just as Pru said. They were on their own horses: Sarge, Bing Cherry, and Marbles. The BUDs were chasing one another around in the arena when they should have been walking to cool down the horses.

"They should be leaving. It's *our* turn," Abigail said.

"I'll talk to them," Lucky told her friends. She hopped on Spirit's back, leaped over the ramada fence, and boldly approached Bebe. "Hey," she said. "We're signed up to use the ramada now."

Abigail and Pru opened the gate and led

their horses into the ramada as well.

Pru said, "Yeah. Chica Linda and I are preparing for a dressage competition next week. We need to practice her piaffe." That was trotting in place. "It's a very complicated move."

"Well, we're not done," Bebe replied. She and Sarge kept trotting around the ring.

Ursula rode over to the PALs atop Bing Cherry. "Come back later," she said.

"First come. First served," Daphne added as she passed. "Or is it the early bird catches the worm? I get those confused."

"I think it's finders keepers, losers weepers," Abigail replied, trying to be helpful. "But you didn't really *find* the ramada, so I don't think you get to keep it."

She pinched her lips together. "And we're not weeping, so we're definitely not the losers here."

"Regardless, it's our turn," Lucky insisted. "We signed up."

Ursula shrugged. "We aren't leaving."

"We need the practice more than you do,"

Daphne agreed. She and Marbles slowed
and approached the group.

"Well, I know that's true"—Lucky
couldn't help smirking—"but your time's
still up." Practice time in the ramada ring
was based on trust and honor.

Bebe finally pulled Sarge over to the

side of the ring. She tightened her grip on his reins. "You can't make us leave," she said.

"But—" Lucky began to argue when suddenly there was shouting behind her. It wasn't Priya and Lyds but rather a mix of boys' voices. Lucky heard Beef, Jack, Alex, and Sahir all talking at once.

"Meatball ate all the hay in the feed bag!" Jack was saying.

"He was hungry," Beef replied testily.

"Then you're supposed to bring in a new bale for the rest of the horses," Jack said.

"I did!" Beef countered. "Meatball ate that, too."

Sahir turned to Alex and said, "*You* left the stall open and Jack's horse, Dusty, popped off for a walkabout. He filled his belly with the apples I was saving for Camilo!"

"Dusty only ate one," Alex protested. "I think Meatball ate the rest." He added that his own horse, Liberty, didn't have any. "Liberty doesn't like apples."

"Meatball shared them with Boomerang," Beef told Alex and Sahir. His voice was loud and echoed through the barn.

"Don't bring Boomerang into this!" Abigail said, riding out of the ramada and over to the boys. "There's no proof he ate Camilo's apples."

Priya stopped debating with Lyds for a moment. She stepped into Boomerang's stall and reached down. When she stood, she held up a forgotten chunk of apple core.

"How do you know that was Camilo's

apple?" Abigail said. "It might have been Scoops's apple."

"My horse didn't have any apples," Lyds said.

"Nor mine," Priya chimed in.

In the ramada and in the barn, everyone was arguing about apples and riding times and hay and tack. The horses were snorting and stomping nervously. The air was filled with yelling and tension.

"Enough!"

The students all went silent as Headmaster Perkins entered the stables. He was riding on his own horse, Horsemaster Jenkins. The headmaster spoke in a low voice, nearly a whisper, so that everyone had to stay quiet in order to hear. Even the horses stilled.

"This will not do." The headmaster's voice was stern. "For the rest of the day, the barn, stables, and ramada will be off-limits. You will all return to your dorm rooms immediately."

"But—" Lucky began. She fully intended to argue for why the PALs deserved to be in the ramada.

"If—" Lyds started to explain what had happened between Priya and her.

"Why—" Beef had a question.

"Maybe—" Alex struggled to tell his point of view.

"No buts," Headmaster Perkins said. "No ifs, no whys, and no maybes." He raised a hand and pointed upstairs to where the students' rooms were located. "My decision

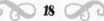

is final. No students are allowed to leave their rooms until further notice."

Horsemaster Jenkins stomped his front hoof with a snort to pass the same message to all the horses.

The students who were on horseback slid down to the ground and quickly put away their tack. Lucky dejectedly slipped off Spirit's back.

The horses quietly returned to their stalls.

"Starting now," Headmaster Perkins declared, "the stables are closed."

Chapter 2

"I'm hungry," Abigail said. "Do you think Lunch Lady Harriet will bring us breakfast this morning?"

The night before, dinner trays had been delivered to the dorm rooms. It was proof that Headmaster Perkins was serious. No students were allowed outside. They were all grounded.

Pru lay on her bunk bed and sighed. "This is the worst! How am I going to be prepared for competition if I can't ride?

Chica Linda doesn't always lead with the correct foot. We have so much work to do!" She moaned. "This stinks."

Abigail opened the dorm room door a crack and sniffed. "Stinks?" she asked. "Stinks like yummy scrambled eggs? Or maybe wonderfully smelly French toast?" She rubbed her belly and peeked outside. "Hi." After some whispering back and forth, Abigail closed the door again.

"Who was out there?" Lucky asked Abigail. Lucky was wearing her riding clothes and pacing the room. If they were allowed to go out, she was ready. Today, they'd get to the ramada first, no matter who was signed up!

"I was talking to Daphne," Abigail said. "She's hungry, too."

"No chatting with the enemy," Lucky said. "We've got to be better prepared to face those ramada snatchers!"

"What if there was a reason they needed more time?" Abigail countered. She flopped down on her own bed. "What if there was a good reason Lyds needed Priya's tack? What if there was a reason Beef gave the hay to Meatball or that Alex left the door open? Maybe we should have listened to one another."

"Nah," Pru said, swinging down off her bed. "Lucky's right. Next time, we'll storm the ramada and take what is rightfully ours."

"I don't think that's—" Abigail began. There was a knock on the door. She forgot what else she was planning to say and instead exclaimed, "Yay! Breakfast."

Abigail rushed to the door and flung it open. There was no one in the hall. No food trays in sight. When she looked down at the floor, there was a letter.

"Oh, sad," Abigail said, frowning at the

envelope. She closed the door. "We can't eat a letter."

"Letter?" Lucky went back to the door and opened it again. She picked up the envelope and held it to the window. "It's an invitation."

"*Ooh*, is it to a party?" Abigail asked, now interested. "I like those little cheese tarts and those hot dogs wrapped in pastry." She closed her eyes in bliss. "Yum."

Lucky opened the envelope and quickly read the invitation. "It's not a party." She passed the card to Pru.

"Good-bye, yummy cheese-tart dreams." Abigail sighed wistfully.

"We're invited to a scavenger hunt," Pru said. "On horseback."

"It's today," Lucky added. "Teams will be made of three horses and their riders. There's a prize for the winning team."

Abigail's tummy rumbled. "A food prize?"

Lucky laughed. "It doesn't say. But do you want to know what it *does* say?"

"No." Abigail frowned. "And I don't care. I can't go on a scavenger hunt until I've had a proper meal."

Pru grinned. "Well then, I have some good news for you. The invitation says we can leave our rooms now. We're going to breakfast!"

"After we eat, Headmaster Perkins will explain the rules of the scavenger hunt," Lucky said.

Abigail cheered. "Breakfast, horseback riding, a scavenger hunt, and prizes—yippee!"

Pru laughed and said, "Maybe today won't be the worst after all."

Chapter 3

"I bet the prize is going to be something amazing!" Lucky said as she waited for Pru and Abigail to saddle their horses. "The PALs *have* to win."

"We will," Pru affirmed as she tightened the cinch strap on Chica Linda's saddle. "I heard that the winning team will get a whole day in the ramada. Chica Linda and I could practice dressage moves all day. No time limits. No sharing. That *would* be amazing."

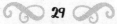

"Spirit and Boomerang would love to help Chica Linda!" Abigail said. "I hope that's the prize." She raised two crossed fingers.

"Well, we heard differently," Bebe said, her voice echoing across the stable. She was busy picking Sarge's hooves clean before the hunt.

"We heard the prize is a campout at the beach," Ursula said as she brushed Bing Cherry's tail. "You all know how we *excel* at camping." Ursula loved reminding the PALs of how they'd met at a Frontier Fillies Summer Outdoor Jubilee. "The BUDs are going to win this scavenger hunt and then enjoy s'mores over a beach bonfire."

"I like to burn the marshmallows for my

s'mores," Daphne added, licking her lips.

"Me too!" Abigail exclaimed. Then, seeing the shocked looks from her friends, she said, "I mean, you won't be able to burn any marshmallows when the PALs win the hunt *and* the s'mores."

Priya; her brother, Sahir; and Beef had formed their own team and were listening to the conversation.

Beef said, "I heard Headmaster Perkins talking to Lunch Lady Harriet this morning. He said that the prize is something no one would ever guess. That's why *I* think it's a trip to the moon."

"Impossible," Priya said, laughing. "*I* think it's private lessons with Coach Bradley. Sahir and I have been asking for time alone with her for ages now. She always says she's slumped." At the others' blank expressions, Priya explained, "She's tired."

"It makes sense to give us something we'd most desire for a prize," Sahir mused. He put on Camilo's bridle.

"I really want to go to the moon," Beef said sadly. After a look from his teammates, he added, "But lessons would be good, too."

Alex, Lyds, and Jack planned to ride as a team. They met the others in the ramada.

"Did you hear what the grand prize is?" Jack asked Lucky.

"You bet we have," Lucky replied. Spirit was breathing heavily, ready for the

adventure to begin. "Hang in there, boy,"
Lucky told her horse. "We'll get started
soon enough."

"Then, you won't be upset when my
team wins," Jack said. "I mean, it's not a
prize you'd ever want."

"Of course we want it," Lucky said,

tossing her head toward Abigail and Pru. "And we're going to win."

"But you don't need new tack," Jack said, staring at Spirit's bare back.

"Tack?" Lucky shook her head. "That's not the prize."

"Of course it is," Lyds said. "Headmaster Perkins knows that I need a new bit and harness. He created this whole game to be able to give it to me without playing favorites."

Alex said, "I'm hoping it's a breast collar. Father said he won't send me a new one for another month." He jingled his spurs in the stirrups. "Mine is worn."

"Tack's not the prize," Lucky insisted. "The real prize is—"

Toot!

Headmaster Perkins blew the starting horn.

Lucky leaned over to her friends and said, "This'll be a piece of cake, PALs!"

"The *BUDs* are going to win," Bebe announced.

"Victory is ours," Sahir told Priya and Beef.

"We'll ride like the relay anchor in a Grand Prix," Alex said to Jack and Lyds. "Get ready!"

Toot! Headmaster Perkins blew his horn again.

"Welcome," he said, "to the first ever Palomino Bluffs Academy team scavenger hunt." He waved his hand toward the students, who were now gathered between two hay bales. This was the starting gate.

"You've been specially chosen for this event," he said.

"I wondered why there aren't other students from school here," Abigail said. She smiled, then cheered. "We were specially chosen! Yay us!"

"Yay, indeed," Headmaster Perkins said with a chuckle. "I see that you've all formed teams on your own. That's nice." He nodded at the riders and their horses. "However, you aren't going to get to choose your own teams today. I will be announcing the new scavenger hunt teams right now."

"Wait, what?" Ursula asked. "But we want to ride with our friends."

"Yes," the headmaster said cryptically. "That's exactly the plan." He pulled a long sheet of paper from his riding vest pocket.

"Pru Granger rides with Bebe Shumann and Jack Ledger," Headmaster Perkins announced.

"*Ooh*, that makes them PB and J!" said Abigail.

"There's been a mistake," Bebe called, raising her hand for attention. "I only ride with the BUDs."

Headmaster Perkins ignored her and continued. "Our second team is Abigail Stone, Lydia Jane Sterling, and Priya Kapoor."

Lyds and Priya stared at each other. They still hadn't made up. Their newest disagreement was about proper cleaning techniques for borrowed tack. That was, of course, for those who had permission to borrow tack.

"Priya, Abigail, and Lyds. The PALs ride together after all," Abigail said, ready to move with Boomerang to join her new teammates.

Lucky stopped her. "Don't go. We'll tell him you can't ride with new PALs."

"You could be the ALP or LAP team

instead," Daphne said, trying to be helpful.

"I hear the ALPs are lovely mountains," Abigail said.

"Lucky Prescott, Ursula Lin Yang, and Sahir Kapoor."

"We are SUL!" Sahir raised his hand to give Ursula a high five.

She turned away, saying, "That's not a word."

Sahir shrugged. "I've never had a team nickname before. I like SUL. It could be a word if we wanted it to be. I am *SUL* happy you are on my team."

Ursula groaned.

"The final group will be Alex Fox, Ben Wellington, and Daphne Visser."

"Oh, that's BAD!" Abigail said to

Daphne, and they both laughed. Then Abigail asked, "Who's Ben?"

"Me," Beef said. "Ben's my real name."

"Oh, just like Lucky's real name is"—she stopped to think about it—"Lucky!"

"Yeah. Sort of like that." Beef grinned.

"Ha-ha! We're BAD to the bone." Alex high-fived Beef. "B-A-D has got this hunt in the B-A-G!"

"It's in the *feed* B-A-G!" Beef joked. They both laughed as if that were the most hysterical thing anyone had ever said.

Coach Bradley rode up quickly and whispered to Headmaster Perkins. "Hold on. There's been a team change," he announced.

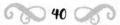

"Thank goodness someone is being reasonable," Ursula said, moving Bing Cherry away from Spirit.

"See ya," Lucky said, and Spirit snorted. "The PALs are back together."

"Not so fast," Headmaster Perkins said. "The change is that Sahir and Beef are switching teams."

Alex grunted, and Beef frowned. They didn't want to be split up.

"Ugh," Daphne told Abigail. "That turns SUL into BUL."

"Or LUB," Abigail suggested. She bit her bottom lip and frowned. "But that's not much better, is it?"

"How about this? I'm *SAD* about the

change," Beef told the girls with a wink.

"That's a good one!" Abigail replied. "Sahir, Alex, and Daphne! Their first names spell SAD!"

"The teams are set," Headmaster Perkins continued. "Gather together with your group, and we will begin."

The students and their horses began rearanging themselves. Before Lucky and Spirit moved to their new team, Lucky told her friends, "If my team wins, I'll still let you both ride in the ramada for the prize."

"If *my* team wins, we'll invite you, too," Pru said.

"If the new PALs win, I won't forget the old PALs," Abigail said, then trotted off with Boomerang to join Priya and Lyds.

"There will never be new PALs," Lucky told Pru. "Ridiculous!"

They both giggled, then went to join their new teams for the scavenger hunt.

Chapter 4

Each team was given a clue in a white envelope. There would be a count of three, and then the teams would be able to open their envelopes and figure out where *this* clue was telling them to go to find the *next* clue. The winners would be the first team to figure out all the clues and return to the school.

"Don't forget," Headmaster Perkins added, "the winning team has to have all

their clue cards to be eligible for the prize."

Lucky opened the clue for her team:

$$Hoof - H + L - OF + G = ?$$

"Huh?" Ursula stared at the clue. "What does that even mean?" She leaned back in Bing Cherry's saddle and complained, "We'll never win if we can't figure out the first clue."

Suddenly, the team of Pru, Bebe, and Jack took off at a gallop. Their horses kicked up dust in the faces of everyone still in the ramada.

"Sorry, Lucky," Pru called out. "Bebe figured it out."

"Working with the enemy," Lucky said under her breath. She stared at the clue harder, as if that would make it clearer.

Abigail's team was the next to hurry out of the arena. "Priya is brilliant," Abigail told Lucky as they darted past. "That's the fancy way of saying 'a smarty-pants.'"

"Follow them!" Ursula said, spurring her horse into action.

"Shouldn't we figure out the clue on

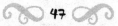

our own?" Lucky asked as Spirit galloped ahead to catch Bing Cherry. "Maybe they're wrong. We could be the only ones going to the correct place!"

"Why bother wasting brain cells?" Ursula replied. She pointed at Daphne and her team. They were galloping out of the ramada. "We don't need to do the hard work—just follow along."

"But we should be certain!" Lucky said. "We can't mess up."

"Then we'll be the first team to figure out the next one," Ursula assured her. "We *will* win."

There was something about the way Ursula said *We* will *win* that made Lucky

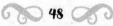

wonder if she was talking about the team with Beef and her or some other team entirely.

"What makes you think *we* can win the scavenger hunt?" Lucky asked as Ursula pulled ahead to pass Sahir, Alex, and Daphne.

"Trust me!" Ursula said, then spurred her horse even harder to catch up with Bebe, Pru, and Jack.

As soon as they entered the forest, Lucky finally figured out the answer to the first clue.

$$Hoof - H + L - OF + G = ?$$

Hoof minus *H* is *oof.*

Plus an *L* is *Loof*.

Subtract *OF* at the end and that leaves only *LO*.

Add a *G*.

All together, the letters left equal *LOG*.

There was a place in the forest where lightning had struck many years earlier and had left about fifteen fallen trees. *Logs*. Lucky was positive that Bebe had figured out the clue correctly. Next time, Lucky would just have to try to figure it out faster.

The groups arrived one after the other to the clearing. Moss-covered logs formed natural horse jumps.

"Now what? How do we find the next clue?" Beef asked. He looked around at all

the logs. "This seems impossible to me."

The teams each moved into their small groups to try to figure out what to do.

Lucky heard Alex tell his group, "Once we find this clue, Grand Prix speed will no longer cut it. We're riding for the Derby cup. The big one! We have the lead now, so let's keep it."

"Good pep talk," Jack said, having overheard. "But you don't have the clue yet, so you're not leading anywhere." He looked around the trees. "We're all equal right now."

"Not for long," Lyds chimed in. She and Scoops began circling the fallen trees, searching for the next clue.

Lucky got off Spirit's back to look inside

any logs that were hollow. She peeked in one to find Abigail staring back at her.

"Find anything?" Abigail asked.

"Nope," Lucky replied. "You?"

"Nope," Abigail said. "I'll go left; you go right. If you find a clue...uh...don't tell me, and I won't tell you."

"Deal," Lucky said with a laugh. She moved on to keep searching.

It was quiet in the forest as everyone searched for the clues. Dark clouds seemed to be gathering overhead, and a gust of wind blew. A minute later, it became bright and sunny again. Lucky mused that the weather on the frontier could be funny at times.

"What if these aren't the right logs?" Pru asked at last. "Maybe we all were wrong, and the clue meant some other logs."

"I only figured out the clue's answer. You're the one who actually brought us here," Bebe said. "That would make it your fault if it's wrong."

"Do you know any other famous logs?" Pru countered. And then she added, "Ramada stealer."

"We already told you: We needed the extra practice time in the ring," Daphne said from a few feet away. "You wouldn't understand."

"Try me," Pru said. "I'm listening."

Daphne looked to Bebe, who shook her head.

Then Alex shouted, "Hey, Beef, old pal, I gotta question."

"I've got answers," Beef replied.

"Why did the horse sneeze?"

"Easy!" Beef chuckled so loudly, it echoed in the trees. "He had hay fever!"

"Thanks, man." Alex gave a signal to his teammates—Sahir and Daphne—and they sped out of the forest.

Before galloping away, Daphne turned

back to Ursula and Bebe. She pointed up at
a tree with low branches. Everyone could
now see new clue cards hanging from long
strings on the twisted branches. It was
obvious that riders had to jump over a fallen
log and grab the hanging cards as they went.

"Thanks, Daph," Ursula said.

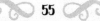

"She's not supposed to help us," Lucky said.

Ursula shrugged. "Do you want the clue or not?"

Jack and Dusty cantered alongside Abigail and Boomerang. They took the jump together, landing in perfect sync. There wasn't enough room for three riders, so Beef and Meatball had to hang back. His team would go last.

"Wanna know what the card says?" Abigail asked Lucky when Boomerang slowed.

"Abigail!" Priya chastised her. "I know it doesn't sound very nice, but I do believe that in this situation, we should not help the enemy."

"Lucky's not the enemy," Abigail said.
Then she realized, "But I guess we want the
prize for ourselves, huh?"

"Yes," Priya said. "Come along now.
We've got a hunt to win."

They were off.

Meatball finally got a chance to safely leap over the log. Beef reached to grab the card for his team then came back to the group to read the clue: "Why did the horse sneeze?" Beef looked up at his teammates and said, "Oops. I accidentally gave the other teams the answer. I didn't know it was the clue's question."

"It's okay, Beef," Lucky told him. "We can ride fast. But do you know where they are all going?"

"Yep," Beef said. "The meadow. Alex, Priya, Jack, and I used to hang out there, but all the flowers gave Meatball hay fever." As if Meatball knew they were talking about him, he sneezed.

Snot and spit splattered over Lucky's leg.

"Gross," she said, wiping the slobber
off her pants. Then she said to Meatball,
"Sounds like you know the way. Meatball,
lead us to the meadow!"

Chapter 5

The large flower-filled meadow was over
a hill behind the school. The colors of the
blooms glistened as Lucky rode Spirit into
the field. Lucky noticed that another dark
cloud passed by overhead. She shivered,
but a moment later, it was sunny once
more.

Meatball sneezed again.

Alex, Sahir, and Daphne had the head
start and got to the meadow first.

When Lucky and her team arrived, Sahir

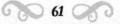

was riding fast toward a bale of hay. His horse, Camilo, took the jump easily. Lucky could see Sahir's head turn as they landed on the far side of the field. He was looking for the clue.

"Nothing here," Sahir reported. "I thought maybe they'd be pinned to the top of the bales. There are four bales. That means four cards."

"It's not going to be the same as the logs," Lucky said. "Headmaster Perkins wouldn't have us do the same jumping trick over and over. There's got to be a different way to find the clue." She stared at the field. Four hay bales had been placed at odd angles.

With a loud "Yeehaw!" Lyds set off at a

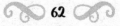

gallop. She rode Scoops around the bales as if they were western barrels.

Scoops was fast. Within seconds, Lyds was back with her team. "No clues are attached to the sides of the hay bales, either."

Lucky noticed that Abigail was staring at her team's last clue card. Her mouth was moving as she silently recited the joke to herself over and over: *Why did the horse sneeze?*

She looked confused. Then she looked surprised. And then Abigail smiled widely.

Lucky rode Spirit over to her friend. "Did you figure out where the clue cards are?"

"I can't tell you," Abigail said. "That wouldn't be fair to my team."

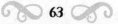

"If I knew the answer, *I'd* tell *you*," Lucky said. "PALs forever, right?"

Abigail said, "I'll be PALs with you again tomorrow." She rode off to join her team and tell them what she'd discovered.

Lucky complained to Spirit. "Why do we have to stay with these new teams? I should be on a team with Pru and Abigail! This isn't fair!"

Ursula overheard. "Yes. I'd rather ride with the BUDs than the BULs any day." She added, "The BUDs would win the prize."

"No. The *PALs* would win," Lucky said.

"You're wrong. The *BUDs* would win," Ursula argued.

"BULs!" Beef called, making Ursula and Lucky both cringe at the new team name. "Abigail's team is moving the hay!"

"Why would they do that?" Lucky asked him.

"She wouldn't tell me, so I snuck up when she was talking to her team!" Beef grinned. "Abigail said that hay fever sounded sick. That made her think of the last time she got a cold. *Cold* rhymes with *mold*. Hay gets moldy if it gets wet. And the best way to dry hay is to move it into the sun." He took a breath from all that and said, "I missed the rest because Meatball sneezed, and we had to sneak away."

Lucky knew how Abigail thought. "Her team is moving a hay bale into a sunnier spot because Abigail thinks the clues are under the hay." She shielded her eyes from the sunlight with one hand to see what was happening.

Across the meadow, Lyds and Priya were working together to wrap a long rope around one of the bales. They tied off the end of the rope to Scoops's saddle horn. After that, they edged the horse forward. Scoops strained as he dragged the bale into the sun.

"Look!" Abigail jumped down off Boomerang and picked up a white card from the ground. "Aha!" she cheered, waving the clue toward her teammates.

Priya and Lyds high-fived. They paused when they realized they were meant to be upset with each other. Abigail said something that Lucky couldn't hear. Then the three rode off to look at the clue in private while the other teams went to move their own bales of hay.

Lucky's team got the next clue quickly. She read it to Ursula and Beef while Meatball sneezed.

"There are six terms on the card: *anvil, rasp, pritchel, calipers, alligator clincher,* and *nippers*. What does that mean?"

"The farrier," Ursula said, glancing around with a suspicious look in her eye. None of the other teams had moved from the meadow. They were all still trying to figure out the clue. "All those things are tools used for shoeing horses. The farrier is the professional horseshoer."

"The farrier's ranch is just over the next hill," Beef said. "Meatball has complicated feet. He gets new shoes more often than I do!"

"See ya later!" Ursula announced. She leaned into Bing Cherry and took off.

"We're coming!" Lucky and Spirit were ready to follow, but were passed by two other riders and their horses.

"What's going on?" Lucky was galloping

fast to catch up with the other riders.

It looked like Ursula had told the clue's answer to the BUDs. The three horses that left the meadow were Bing Cherry, Sarge, and Marbles!

Lucky rounded back and hurried over to Pru and Abigail. "Come on! The PALs need to go together if we want to beat the BUDs to the farrier's ranch."

There was a moment of confusion when all the teams didn't know what to do. Did they leave their assigned groups and join up with their best friends? Or did they stay in the groups that Headmaster Perkins had told them to work with?

After a few moments, they all split up.

"Let's go!" Lucky told her friends. Spirit,

Chica Linda, and Boomerang took off toward the farrier's ranch together.

Lucky smiled.

The PALs—*her* PALs—were going to win the scavenger hunt!

Chapter 6

Priya and Sahir were the fastest riders at school. But they didn't get a good head start. The PALs arrived at the farrier's ranch right behind the BUDs.

Lucky saw Ursula leaving the farrier's shed with white cards in her hand.

Lucky dropped from Spirit's back and ran to the shed. The door was open. The farrier wasn't there.

"We have to find the next clue!" she told

Pru and Abigail when they entered.

"The BUDs are probably solving it right now," Priya said. She and Sahir had arrived. Beef was with them. They'd left the horses in the farrier's field and come inside.

The toolshed was made of wood with a tin roof. It smelled like dust, charcoal, and metal. A sudden wind blew hard. The roof rattled. Lucky glanced out the door, but besides a few gathering clouds, there was no sign of bad weather.

She focused on finding the clue. "Where is it?" Lucky muttered.

Shelves lined the walls. There were tools of every kind hanging from hooks and spread out on a heavy wooden workbench.

Horseshoes in all sizes were stacked in labeled boxes. There was a cold box tucked in the corner. When lit, it would be a fire forge, used for heating a horseshoe before bending it into the perfect fit for each horse's hoof.

Lyds, Alex, and Jack were the last three in the shed. It was suddenly crowded in the small space. Everyone was pushing and growing louder as they tried to find the remaining clues.

"I detest small spaces," Priya said. Her face was pink. She was gasping for air. "*And* I don't function well in crowds. I must go outside." She tried moving through the other students toward the exit when, suddenly, the door to the tiny shed slammed shut, closing them all inside.

Lyds rushed over, stepping on Beef's toes as she went. "Sorry!"

"I'm okay!" he said with a thumbs-up.

Priya pressed against the door. "Oh goodness, it won't open. We're locked in!"

"The horses are all outside!" Alex said, looking through a small dusty window at the back of the shed. He called, "Hey, Liberty, set us free!" His horse snorted and went to stand between Spirit and Meatball.

"It's the BUDs," Lyds said. "I know that they're behind this. I think they took all the clues and locked us in so we couldn't follow them."

Lucky had seen Ursula with a handful of cards, but she knew that didn't mean Ursula had taken all the clues. She'd need more proof.

"I bet they're already back at school, finished with the entire scavenger hunt," Jack said.

"And enjoying the prize." Pru sighed.

"We don't have any proof the BUDs locked us in," Lucky said. She loved detective stories. This felt like a mystery.

"And we don't know if the clues were really in here," Abigail added.

Jack said, "We know the BUDs broke up the groups to be together. We also know they will do anything to win the scavenger hunt without the rest of us." He slammed his fist against the shed door. "Now there are no clue cards *and* we're trapped."

"Trapped!" Priya moaned. "It's stifling hot in here. I can't breathe!" She tried to kick open the shed door, but it wouldn't budge. Priya was clearly getting more and more nervous.

"I'm concerned," Sahir said. "Priya's usually got a lovely disposition. Something is terribly wrong."

"I know what to do." Lyds guided Priya to close her eyes and not think about the small space they were in. "You're an expert in dressage. Can you tell me what a free walk is?"

"Of course," Priya said between heavy breaths. "It's when a horse takes long, rhythmic strides."

"Great," Lyds told her. "We're going to do a free walk with your breathing." She showed Priya how to do it. "Inhale very slowly. Exhale very slowly. Count to make them even."

"I can do that." Priya nodded and started to breathe. Little by little, she began to calm down.

When she felt better, Priya said to Lyds, "Thank you, Lyds. That was impressive. How'd you know what I needed?"

"Yesterday, I wrote an article about what to do in emergencies." She sighed. "Priya, I'm sorry I used your tack," Lyds told her. "Scoops's harness broke, and the newspaper deadline was ten minutes away. If I didn't get to the *Trotter* office on time, no one would ever read what I learned about how to handle bad situations. I borrowed your tack so I could ride to the newspaper office. I should have asked." Lyds continued, "I forgot to clean it. That was my fault. Can you forgive me?"

"Your article helped me!" Priya leaned

over and hugged Lyds. "You can borrow my tack anytime. Bring it back dirty—I don't mind at all." She added, "Thank you again."

"It's what friends do," Lyds said.

"Good friends," Priya said with a smile.

"I'm sorry about the hay," Beef told Jack. "I really was going to get more for the feed bag, but I got distracted. Meatball had lain down and wouldn't get up. I was so worried he had colic that I forgot to get the hay. Then the vet came. She said that Meatball had a terrible tummy ache from eating so much!" He plugged his nose and added with a laugh, "I never knew a horse could have so much gas!"

"No worries," Jack said. "Horse health comes first. I get it."

"And I knew the stall door was busted," Alex told Sahir. "I went to get a screwdriver to fix it. Dusty got out while I was gone. I'm sorry about the apples." He said to Jack, "And I'm sorry I let your horse out, too."

"Mistakes happen," Sahir said. "There are always more apples on the tree."

"See?" Abigail said. "Everyone had a reason for everything that happened. If only we'd talked to one another instead of arguing."

Pru said, "Except for the BUDs. They still shouldn't have been in the ramada during our session."

"And they shouldn't have locked us in here," Jack said. He looked around for a key to the door. "What are we going to do? We can't stay here forever."

There was a howl of wind. Hard rain began to fall. The sound of it hitting the tin roof was loud.

"Oh my, oh my!" Priya started gasping. "Someone needs to get us out of here before lightning strikes the shed!"

Suddenly, the shed door began to rattle.

"Lucky? Pru? Abigail?" It was Bebe's voice.

"Sahir? Priya? Jack?" That was Daphne.

"Beef? Alex? Lyds?" Ursula pounded on the door.

"Are you all in there?" Bebe shook the shed knob again. "You have to let us in! It's raining cats and dogs."

"Please," Daphne begged urgently. "Hail is splattering all around us. The sky is a

scary green color." Her voice was panicked. "I think a tornado is coming!"

"*You* locked us in," Jack said. "Open the door yourselves!"

Daphne cried, "We didn't lock you in! We saw the wind blow it shut. We can't pull it open!"

Lucky told the others, "See? One mystery is solved." Then she asked Bebe about the other mystery. "Where are the clue cards?"

"We hid them in the cold box," Bebe admitted through the door. "Headmaster Perkins said you had to have the clue cards to win, and the cards were just lying on the table, not even hidden. It was too easy!"

"We thought we'd rush back to school after we figured out the last clue," Ursula shouted through the shed door. "No other team would have a chance because they wouldn't find the clue in time."

"You can have *all* the clues! Take ours," Daphne shouted against a howling wind. "Just let us in." She added, "Please."

A clue card slid under the door. Lucky picked it up. The card had a picture of a horse and an arrow pointing to where a saddle would be.

"What does this mean?" Lucky asked her friends.

"The arrow is pointing at the horse's back," Pru said. "Maybe the answer is Spirit, since you're the one who rides bareback?"

"I think—" Alex started.

"Can you guess later?" Bebe cried out.

"It's dangerous out here!" Ursula shouted over a booming thunder strike.

Lucky looked to Pru and Abigail and said, "We have to do something."

"How are we going to help?" Pru said. "We can't get the shed door open. The wind is too strong."

Lucky looked out the small shed window. Even if they broke the glass, the frame was too small for a person to squeeze through. In the field, she could see Spirit and the other horses gathered together, protecting one another from the now constant blowing wind. Their backs were to the storm.

"Spirit!" Lucky called to her horse. But Spirit couldn't hear her; the wind was too loud.

"Help us!" Bebe shouted again.

Her voice faded as the shed shook and a loud crashing sound echoed all around them.

"Oh no!" Alex shouted. "The roof!" The tin roof had partially blown off with the last

gust of wind, and there was a big hole in the middle. The shed creaked and groaned. Rain was coming inside, making everything wet.

"Get back!" Lucky shouted to Bebe, Ursula, and Daphne. "Get as far away from the shed as you can."

Priya cried out, "First we were going to suffocate. Now we're going to be smashed!"

"Take more free-walking breaths," Lyds reminded her.

"I'll try," Priya said. "It's a challenge, but I will imagine I'm in the dressage arena, riding atop Tiger Lily." She squeezed her eyes shut.

"We have to get out of here." Lucky went

back to the window to call Spirit again.
When she peeked out, she was surprised
to find his big eyes staring back at her. "It's
Spirit," Lucky said. "And he brought the
others."

All the horses had gathered outside the
shed.

Pru and Abigail swept everything off
the farrier's worktable and moved it to the
center of the shed, under the gaping hole in

the roof. They waited until there wasn't any lightning. Then, one by one, the students began to climb out.

Since Bebe, Ursula, and Daphne were already outside, they held the horses steady.

First Priya pulled herself out of the hole and slid down the side of the shed. Then Jack and Alex. Next Sahir and Lyds.

"Spirit found a cave!" Bebe reported. "It's just on the other side of the farrier's shed. He's leading everyone there."

The horses carried their riders to safety in turn.

Lucky, Pru, Abigail, and Beef were the last ones left in the shed.

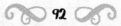

The wind was swirling, and from the sky, hail the size of small rocks pounded down onto the tin roof, clattering even more loudly than the rain.

Through the little window, Lucky could see the tornado that Daphne had reported. It was swirling toward them, destroying everything in its path.

"Hurry!" Lucky shouted over the booming weather. "We have to get out of here."

Beef told Pru, "You go next. I'll boost you up; I'll escape after."

"The PALs always go together," Pru said. "It's your turn, Beef! Get on Meatball and ride to the cave." He protested at first, insisting he'd wait for the PALs. But they convinced him to go. A moment later, Meatball carried him away from the shed.

Lucky, Pru, and Abigail all stood on the farrier's table, looking out the hole in the roof. Nearby, Spirit, Chica Linda, and Boomerang waited for them to climb down what was left of the roof.

Lucky reached up to pull herself onto the

94

roof. Suddenly, a huge gust of wind blew hard, and the edge of the tornado swirled onto the shed.

"Run, Spirit!" she shouted. "Take Chica Linda and Boomerang to the cave. Be safe!"

Lucky jumped off the farrier's table. Pru and Abigail jumped down, too, and they all ducked under the workbench. "The safest place in the shed is away from the window and under something heavy that won't blow away," Lucky said.

"Let's hold on to the legs to add extra weight in case the wind picks it up," Pru told her friends.

"I'm closing my eyes," Abigail said, "and taking slow breaths like Lyds taught Priya."

She wrapped her arms around one of the table legs.

Lucky shut her eyes tight, too.

They all breathed in and out together.

The wind whistled. The tornado swirled, and an instant later, the whole shed blew away.

Chapter 7

"Is it over?" Abigail asked once the world quieted.

They were sitting outside, in the spot where the shed used to be. The only thing left was the table they sat under.

The wind had stopped blowing. The rain had stopped falling.

As quickly as the storm clouds had appeared, they disappeared.

"We're okay," Pru said, standing up. She checked her friends. No one was hurt.

The PALs looked out toward the cave that had protected their classmates.

Bebe stepped into the sunlight and gave them a wave. It meant that everyone was all right there, too.

"Whew," Lucky said. She stood and shook dirt and leaves off her clothing. Everything was damp, and rainwater dripped from her hair. The sun was out now. It was warm, and they'd soon all be dry.

"That was too close," Abigail said. "I don't want to meet another tornado. Ever."

"Me neither," Pru said.

Everyone from the scavenger hunt teams gathered around where the shed used to be. The clue cards from the hunt were scattered all over the ground, along with the farrier's tools.

"Let's clean up," Pru suggested. "We can gather the cards and make sure everything looks at least a little okay when the farrier comes back."

As they started to clean, the BUDs made sure to give Abigail all the clue cards.

Abigail was putting them in piles when she noticed something strange. "Look!" She called everyone together. "On the back of each card is a word."

"We'd only been reading the part with the clues," Jack said.

"We didn't know there was more on the other side!" Beef said.

"That's what the last clue was trying

to tell us," Lyds said. "Back! The arrow pointing to the horse's back meant to look at the back of the cards!"

Abigail lay the cards upside down on the farrier's workbench. Together, they formed a message.

Beef read the first three cards: "'Knowst ruefri theherd.'"

Jack added, "*Endship* is the word on the back of the clues that the BUDs found here."

"That doesn't make any sense," Alex said.

"It makes total sense," Daphne said. She came over and shifted the words so that the cards were one next to the other. It looked like this: theherdknowstruefriendship

Abigail mentally added the correct spaces and said, "The herd knows true friendship."

"What does that even mean?" Beef asked. "The herd? What herd?"

Ursula pointed to their horses. "When

the tornado came, our horses found the cave, then gathered everyone together for protection."

"They took care of one another," Daphne said.

"The herd knows true friendship," Priya repeated.

"And they took care of us as if we were part of the herd as well." Jack reached out to rub his horse's nose. "When we were all inside the cave, they stood in a tight circle around us."

Spirit laid his head against Lucky's neck.

"I think we should tell Headmaster Perkins that we *all* won the scavenger hunt," Bebe said.

"People and horses, too!" Sahir said.

"Everyone deserves the prize!"

"We're the Palomino Bluffs Academy herd," Lyds said. She mounted her horse and waited for the others.

"Let's go find Headmaster Perkins." Pru and Chica Linda led the way.

On the way back to school, Daphne told Abigail, "Maybe we could call our new herd something with all our names. Like, APPLAUD...or BURLAP..." Daphne frowned. "There are too many of us. I can't make a word with everyone's names."

"I got it! We're PBJALPSULBAD," said Abigail.

"That's not a word," Daphne said.

"It is now," Abigail told her.

They both laughed.

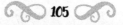 105

Chapter 8

"I'm very impressed with you all," said Headmaster Perkins. At the first sign of the tornado, he'd sent a team of teachers out on horseback to find the students. But the students came back to school safely all on their own.

"I was simply hoping you'd discover a way to work together," the headmaster continued. "The mystery quote was meant to be about how horses are friends. I thought that maybe you could be like the

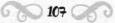

horses." He grinned widely, ear to ear. "But you did even better. You formed your own herd. Herds protect one another, like family." He looked at the students and announced, "Bebe and Sahir told me you all deserve the prize. I agree!"

"Is it lessons with Coach Bradley?" Priya asked.

"Or time in the ramada?" Pru wondered.

"If it's not a trip to the moon, could it be snacks?" Beef said. He added, "Maybe some extra hay and apples for the horses, too?" He put his arms around Alex and Sahir.

Lucky glanced up at the sky. The dark clouds that had turned into a tornado were gone now. A rainbow stretched over the school.

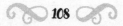

"*Ooh,*" Abigail said. "I bet the rainbow is the prize!"

"Headmaster Perkins couldn't make a rainbow just for us," Lucky said. "Rainbows appear after rain!"

"I still think it's the prize," Abigail said.

"Well," Headmaster Perkins said with a chuckle, "if you *want*, I can always tell Lunch Lady Harriet to put back the ice-cream sundaes I had planned."

"No!" Abigail blurted out. She said, "We can have two prizes."

"In that case, you need to solve one last one." Headmaster Perkins handed out new clue cards. "This clue will lead you to the ice-cream sundaes!"

The first thing Lucky did was turn it over to the back. There was nothing there. They'd solved the friendship puzzle and come out better than ever. A new herd. A school herd. She smiled.

Abigail carefully read the card out loud.

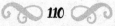

"'Bit, equine, alfalfa, comb, halter.'"

"What does that mean?" Beef asked.

Lucky leaped up on Spirit's back. She was ready to ride. "I know the answer!"

But she wasn't the only one who got it. Quick as a blink, Abigail was on Boomerang and Pru mounted Chica Linda.

The other riders figured it out as well.

But this time, no one rushed. They all waited patiently for Lyds, who was the last rider to guess the clue.

"Don't tell me...," she said, staring at the card. She said the words slowly. "Bit, equine, alfalfa, comb, halter." She frowned, then said, "Can I get a hint?"

"It's like PBJALPSULBAD," Abigail told her.

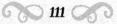

"Oh!" Lyds cheered. "I know where to go!"

In a flash, the group took off together to the beach.

"It was like what Abigail did with our names," Lyds said while they rode toward the stretch of sand. "The first letter of

each word solved the puzzle: *B* for bit, *E* for equine, *A* for alfalfa, *C* for comb, *H* for halter."

Bebe rode next to Lucky. "I bet you want to know why we needed more time in the ramada."

"You know, I don't think I do. If you

say you had a reason, I'm sure it was an important one," Lucky said. "We're okay now. All is forgiven."

"I assure you it was," Bebe said with a wink. "But next time we're riding in the ring, you can have an extra five minutes of our time. Fair is fair." She and the BUDs trotted ahead.

Lucky rode the rest of the way to the beach with Pru and Abigail.

Lunch Lady Harriet was standing in the sand. She had a long table set with ice cream, chocolate syrup, marshmallow fluff, and cherries for the top. The students dismounted and gathered around the table, chattering pleasantly.

"Friends fight sometimes," Pru told

Lucky as she chose her sundae flavors.

"But we always make up," Lucky said, nibbling a cherry.

Abigail grinned. "And this is the best way to make up," she said, piling scoops of sprinkles on her whipped cream. "Deliciously!"

Stacia Deutsch is the *New York Times* bestselling author of more than 300 children's books. Her favorite books are mysteries, movie novelizations, time-travel adventures, and horse stories, of course! Stacia lives in California with her husband, two dogs, three kids, four horses, and a lot of wild bunnies. You can visit her at **www.staciadeutsch.com** or find her on Facebook, Twitter, or Instagram.

Born in La Plata, Argentina, **Maine Diaz** grew up drawing and painting. Cartoons captured her imagination early on, and she realized immediately that she wanted to be an animator when she grew up. At the age of sixteen, Maine took a workshop and started animating. Soon after, she started illustrating for children's storybooks and educational books.

Currently, Maine lives in a tiny green house, where she spends time with her two cats, Chula and Lola. When not illustrating, she enjoys swimming, writing, and taking photos.

ALL NEW EXPERIENCES!

NETFLIX | NOW STREAMING

ALL NEW ADVENTURES!